Deleted

For St. Barnabas
C.E. V.C. Primary
School with love
V.F.

For Kevin and Luis
P.A.

Vivian French's retelling of
"Why the Sea Is Salt" is based on
a Norwegian folk tale first collected
by Peter Christen Asbjörnsen
and Jörgen I. Moe
in the 1840s.

Text copyright © 1993 by Vivian French
Illustrations copyright © 1993 by Patrice Aggs

First U.S. edition 1993
Published in Great Britain in 1993
by Walker Books Ltd., London.
Library of Congress Cataloging-in-Publication Data:
French, Vivian.
Why the sea is salt / retold by Vivian French;
illustrated by Patrice Aggs.
Summary: A retelling of the Norwegian folktale
in which a magical churn repays a young girl's
generosity and her mean uncle's greed.
[1. Folklore—Norway.] I. Aggs, Patrice, ill. II. Title.
PZ8.1.F8885Wh 1993   92-53138
398.21—dc20   [E]
ISBN 1-56402-183-1

10 9 8 7 6 5 4 3 2 1

Printed in Hong Kong

The pictures in this book were done in
watercolor and pen line.

Candlewick Press
2067 Massachusetts Avenue
Cambridge, Massachusetts 02140

WHY THE SEA IS SALT

BY
VIVIAN FRENCH

ILLUSTRATED BY
PATRICE AGGS

CANDLEWICK PRESS
CAMBRIDGE, MASSACHUSETTS

Long ago there was a wide and rolling sea that lipped and lapped at the toes of a little gray town. The sea was as blue and as green as a kingfisher's wing, and if you dipped and dabbled a hand in its sparkling waters, you would find that the drops on your fingers tasted as sweet as the water from a mountain stream.

Behind the little gray town was a small hill, and on the small hill was a little house. On the other side of the valley was a high hill, and on the high hill was a tall house. In the tall house lived a tall, lean man. He was very rich, with a cellar full of gold and silver, and kitchens full of puddings and pies and peaches and cream.

In the little house lived a tiny woman with her seventeen children. They had no money at all, and their kitchen was quite empty, except for a pile of empty plates and a cobweb in the corner.

"What are we going to have for Christmas?" the children asked their mother one day. "Are we going to have presents? A tree? A turkey?"

The tiny woman shook her head. "There's nothing to be had, my lovelies. I have nothing left in my pocket but a pebble, and there's nothing in my purse but a hole."

"Can't we ask our fine uncle up on the high hill to help us?" asked the oldest daughter. "He's got more than enough for all of us, and some more to spare besides."

"Oh no, Matilda," said the tiny woman. "My brother was mean as a boy, and he's mean as a man. He won't give us a crumb for Christmas."

"But there's no harm in asking," said Matilda, putting on her shawl. "We won't be any worse off if he says no—and if he says yes, then we'll have a merry Christmas."

Matilda ran down the small hill, and trudged up the high hill.

The door knocker was huge and heavy, and when Matilda lifted it and let it drop again the sound echoed and clanged all around her. The door opened slowly and heavily.

"Who is it?" asked Matilda's uncle in a deep, dark voice.

"It's me, Uncle," said Matilda.

"Christmas is coming, and we have nothing at all in the house except a pile of empty plates and a cobweb in the corner of the kitchen, so I thought that you might help us."

"Why?" asked the uncle.

Matilda scratched her head. "Well, perhaps because you're so kind?"

"I'm not," said the uncle.

"Ah," said Matilda. "Maybe you feel sorry for us?"

"No," said the uncle.

"But you are our uncle," said Matilda.

The uncle stepped forward.

"Did I ever ask your mother to have seventeen children?"

"Well, no, I don't suppose you ever did," Matilda said.

"And did I ever ask you to waste all your money on eating and drinking?"

"We did need to eat," said Matilda, "but you certainly didn't ask us to."

"And did I ever ask to be your uncle?"

"Well, no, I don't suppose you ever asked that either," Matilda said.

"Then," said the uncle, "I don't see why I should give you so much as a crumb for Christmas."

"That's what my mother said you'd say," said Matilda, turning to go. "But I said that there's no harm in asking. I'll wish you a merry Christmas and hurry off home."

"Just a minute!" The uncle turned and stamped away into his house. Matilda waited on the doorstep.

What has he gone to get? she wondered. Biscuits? Ice cream? Peppermints? Plums?

"Here you are." Her uncle was back, holding a plain green bottle and a brown paper package. "And don't you ever come bothering me again."

Matilda took the bottle and the package.

"Thank you very much, dear Uncle," she said. "Wouldn't you like to eat Christmas dinner with us?"

"I would not," said the uncle, and he slammed the door shut.

Matilda began to run down the hill. Then she walked. Then she stopped.

"I wonder what's in the bottle?" she said to herself. "And what's in the package?"

Very carefully she opened the bottle. Very carefully she sniffed it. Then, very carefully, she tasted it.

"Oh," Matilda said. "Water." She sighed.

Very slowly she untied the string around the package. Very slowly she unwrapped the paper.

"Ugh," Matilda said. "Dried bacon."

"Ahem!"

"What?" Matilda turned around.

A rusty, dusty old man stood just behind her.

"Begging your pardon, my dearie—but could I ask you for a bite to eat and a drop to drink?"

"There's never any harm in asking," said Matilda, "and you're more than welcome—but it's only water and some cold dried bacon."

The old man took a drink and a slice of meat. He chewed carefully for a long time, and then he nodded his head.

"Thank you kindly, my dear, my deario. Now—do you have a fine feast for Christmas?"

"Not exactly," Matilda said. "Only the bacon."

"Then listen to me. Do you have a long memory?"

"Yes, I do. I'm very good at remembering things," Matilda said.

"Good—that's good, my deario. Now, take your meat and water, and go through the woods to the darkest door. Knock three times and, whatever is offered to you say, 'I want the churn behind the door.' Take nothing else."

"I want the churn behind the door," Matilda repeated.

"Then you must hurry home. And remember one more thing—hip hop, little churn, hip hop stop!"

"I'll remember," said Matilda. "But what's a churn?"

"One, two, three, just wait and see!" There was a puff of wind, and Matilda sneezed. When she looked up, the little old man was nowhere to be seen.

Matilda ran down the high hill and into the woods. In and out of the trees she hurried, looking around her. "Where's the darkest door?" she asked herself. "Where should I look?"

The trees were growing taller and darker. There was a rustling and a stirring as the wind began to blow.

"Ooooooh!" Matilda shivered.

A gust of wind blew a branch aside, and Matilda saw a door. It was the darkest door she had ever seen. Matilda shivered again.

"I want the churn behind the door," she said to herself. "Well, there's no harm in asking."

Matilda knocked once.

Nothing happened.

Matilda knocked again, louder.

No one answered.

She knocked again, as loudly as she could.

The door burst open with a crash that shook the ground under Matilda's feet. A dark, dark shadow swirled out through the doorway and glared at Matilda with red and staring eyes. Then it sniffed, and it snorted, and it sniffed again.

"Meat," it growled, "and water? GIVE THEM TO ME!"

Matilda held on tightly to the green bottle and the brown paper package, and shook her head.

"I'll give you gold! Mountains of gold!" shouted the shadow.

Matilda tried to speak, but her voice seemed to have dried up into a little squeak.

"I want the churn behind the door," she whispered.

"MOUNTAINS AND RIVERS OF RUBIES AND GOLD!"

Black smuts of soot blew into Matilda's face. She coughed and stamped her foot.

"I want the churn behind the door!"

There was a rush of wind, and the shadow towered above her holding something that looked like a barrel. Throwing it on the ground in front of Matilda, it snatched the green bottle and the piece of dried bacon from her hands. The meat sizzled and scorched black, and the water bubbled and boiled and gave off a cloud of steam. The door shut with an echoing clang.

Matilda rubbed her eyes and looked around her. She was standing alone among the trees. There was a faint smell of burning in the air, but she could see no sign of a door at all.

She looked at the wooden barrel.

"So this is a churn," she said. "It looks very ordinary—just like a little barrel on legs, with a handle. I don't see what's so special about it."

Matilda picked up the churn and began to carry it back home. It was very heavy and awkward in her arms, and at the bottom of the little hill she sat down with a flump.

"I wish I'd kept the meat and water," she said crossly. "This churn is too heavy. I wish I had something to drink."

The churn began to tremble and shake. Matilda's eyes grew wide as the handle slowly turned all by itself—*chinkelly chunk, chunkelly chink*. The top of the churn flew

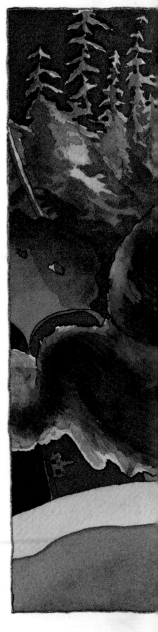

open and water began to pour out in a silvery stream.

Matilda tried to catch it in her hands, but it splashed between her fingers.

"OH! OH! OH!" she said.

The churn went on turning. *Chinkelly chunk, chunkelly chink,* it went. Matilda's feet were getting wet, and a shining lake was widening over the grass.

"Stop! Stop!" Matilda called. "That's plenty! Please stop!"

The churn went on turning.

"I thought you had a long memory," said a rusty voice in Matilda's ear.

"Of course!" she cried, clapping her hands. "I remember!" She leaned toward the churn. "Hip hop, little churn, hip hop stop!"

The churn stopped. Matilda began to laugh. All the water was sinking into the ground and she still had nothing to drink.

"I think I'd better go home," she said.

Matilda's mother and her brothers and sisters were waiting at the door of the house. When they saw Matilda coming they waved and shouted, and came running out to help her. "What is it? What is it?" they all asked at once. "It's our Christmas dinner," Matilda said. "Just watch." She patted the churn. "Please may we have a Christmas dinner?" *Chinkelly chunk, chunkelly chink.* Out of the churn came a tablecloth, flapping and floating through the air. It settled on the table, and was followed by knives and forks and spoons and cups and plates. Then came all the most wonderful things to eat that Matilda and her brothers and sisters had ever dreamed of, and a great many things that they had never thought of at all. Last of all came a pudding—a steaming plum pudding—with blue flames flickering over it and a sprig of holly on the top.

"OOOOOH!" said all the children. Matilda smiled happily. "Hip hop, little churn, hip hop stop!" she whispered.

From that day on Matilda and her family were very happy. Whenever they needed anything they asked the churn, and the handle turned around and around until they had enough. They had five red hens, six fat sheep, seven plump pigs, and eight black-and-white cows.

Up on the high hill the uncle watched and wondered.

"They said they had nothing but a pile of plates and a cobweb in the corner," he said to himself. "Where have these hens and sheep and pigs and cows come from?"

He pulled on his big black hat, swung his black cloak around his shoulders, and set off down the high hill and up the small hill. When he reached the little house, he strode in through the front door without so much as a knock on the door, and Matilda's tiny mother and all the children jumped up in surprise.

"Why, fancy seeing you, Brother!"

said the mother. "Sit down, do, and let us tell you all about our good fortune." She patted the churn.

"Dear churn, make us a fine tea."

The uncle's eyes grew bigger and bigger as the handle slowly began to turn. His mouth fell open as tea and cake and toast and jam floated out, up into the air and onto the table. He was so busy staring that he didn't notice at all when Matilda crept close to the churn and whispered, "Hip hop, little churn, hip hop stop."

"Our clever Matilda found it for us last Christmas," said the tiny woman. "She bargained for it with a piece of cold dried bacon and a bottle of water."

"What?" roared the uncle, leaping to his feet.

Matilda's mother nodded. "Indeed she did, and what a fine thing it was for us all."

The uncle folded his arms.

"Just tell me," he growled, "who it was that gave Matilda that piece of meat?"

"Why, Brother dear, it was you!" The tiny woman patted his arm.

"And who," the uncle asked, "gave Matilda that bottle of water?"

The tiny woman smiled happily. "Why, Brother, you again! And very kind of you it was."

"Then," said the uncle with a greedy grin, "that churn is rightfully MINE!"

He snatched up the churn, tucked it under his arm, and marched out of the house. The tiny woman burst into tears.

"Don't cry, Mother," Matilda said. "Let's just wait for a little while and see what happens." And she went to sit on the step outside the house.

The uncle carried the churn down the small hill. As he went striding up the high hill it grew heavier and heavier, and when the uncle

reached his hallway he put it down with a grunt.

"Humph," the uncle said. "Now, what should I start with? I know! Something to eat. And then I will set you to work, little churn—churning gold until my cellars are full and running over. Maybe I will build another barn to house my gold, and then another, and another, but now—I'll have porridge!" The uncle slapped the churn. "PORRIDGE! Oh, and while you're at it, I'll have a couple of fine fresh fish, and hurry up about it."

The churn's handle began to jerk and twitch. Then—*chinkelly chunk, chunkelly chink*—it turned around and around, faster and faster. Porridge came pouring out in a thick sticky stream, and fish popped out and flapped onto the ground in twos and threes, tens and twenties, forties and fifties.

"STOP!" roared the uncle. "That's enough!"

But the churn did not stop. On and on it churned, and the porridge sucked and squelched around the uncle's feet, then his ankles, then his knees. Fish were heaped in piles all around him until the hallway was so full that they spilled out of the door and down the path.

The uncle shouted and growled and stamped and ranted, but it did no good. On and on went the churn—*chinkelly chinkelly chunk, chunkelly chunkelly chink*. At last the uncle began to wade down the hill, pushing heavily through the rising tide of porridge and fish.

"HELP!" bellowed the uncle. "HELP!" Matilda looked up from her seat on the step. She saw her uncle coming, and smiled a small secret smile.

"HELP!" Her uncle was red in the face and puffing and panting as he hurried toward Matilda. "HELP!"

"What is it, Uncle?" Matilda asked, getting up.

"I'm being drowned in porridge and fish," he gasped. "You must stop that churn, and then I'll chop it up for firewood!"

"Oh," said Matilda. She sat down again.

"What are you doing? You must come NOW, this very minute!" the uncle shouted angrily.

"Well, I think I'd like to have my little churn back," Matilda said. "So if I stop the porridge, may I bring the churn home?"

"ANYTHING! JUST HURRY!" The uncle was turning from red to purple.

Matilda skipped down the hill. As she climbed up the high hill, porridge swirled around her, and she saw that her uncle's house was slowly disappearing in a lake of porridge.

Matilda reached the hallway and seized the churn.

"Hip hop, my clever little churn," she said, "hip hop stop."

The churn stopped, and Matilda held it tightly as she slid and slithered back down the hill to her home. The uncle, staggering back up the high hill once more, shook his fist at the churn.

"My beautiful house! My cellars of gold! My puddings and pies and peaches and cream!" he wailed as he looked in his front door. "Ruined! All ruined!"

Matilda and her family had a celebration supper. Then they went on living very happily, apart from the days when the sun shone very strongly and the wind blew from the east. On those days there was a faint but unmistakable smell of fish, and Matilda's tiny mother sent the children around the house to close all the windows.

"Maybe we should move?" suggested Matilda.

"Maybe we should," said her tiny mother, and the sixteen other children clapped their hands.

"Could we live by the sea?" asked the littlest child.

Matilda nodded. "I know just the house," she said.

Matilda and her mother and all the sixteen children moved into a tall white house on the edge of the harbor, and every day they watched the sparkling waters of the sea lapping at the toes of the little gray town. They watched the tall ships coming in and out, and loading and unloading their goods, and they were very happy. Matilda liked to sit on a pile of rocks at the harbor's entrance and dabble her fingers in the clean, clear water.

She was sitting there one day when a fine white ship came cutting through the waves and tied up just beside her. A tall lean man in a black hat and a black cloak came hurrying down the gang-

plank, holding a large white hankie to his eyes and weeping and wailing and crying and sobbing.

"What is it?" Matilda asked. "Can I help you?"

"Dear child," said the man from behind his hankie. "Have pity on a poor sailor with nothing left in the world but sixteen sad sisters and a pile of empty plates and a cobweb in the corner of the kitchen."

"Oh dear!" said Matilda, "I'm so very sorry—I know just how you feel. Oh!" She jumped up. "Wait here!"

Matilda hurried along the harbor wall and into her house. She found the churn and carried it back to where the poor sailor was snuffling into his hankie.

"Here," Matilda said. "Somebody gave this to me when I had nothing, and now I have everything I could ever want. Please take it. It will bring you good fortune, too."

Matilda stopped. The sailor wasn't listening to her. He was hurrying away with the churn, back toward the fine ship, and as Matilda watched, he jumped on board and began hauling up the anchor. The sails filled in the breeze, and the ship swept away over the wide and rolling sea.

"Dear me," said Matilda. "And I never told him how my little churn works." She walked slowly back to her house.

On board the ship, the sailor, who was really Matilda's uncle, was rubbing his hands together.

"This time," he gloated, "I will make sure that I fill my houses and cellars and barns with gold—yes, and with rubies, too. This time the churn will make me the richest man in the world. I will start it churning, churning, churning, and no matter to me if it never stops again—indeed, if it churns for ever and ever, so much the better."

Carrying the churn, the uncle went down into a magnificent cabin decorated with red and silver. The captain met him in the doorway. "So, where's your treasure?" he asked, staring at the little wooden churn. "What? What? What? All the promises you made me, all the gold you said you'd give me—all for an old barrel?"

The uncle smiled a sly, greedy smile. "Just wait until your fine tall ship brings me to shore again," he said. "Then all my debts and more will be fully repaid. Now, is my meal ready?"

The captain nodded.

The uncle sat down at a table laid with dishes of silver. There were puddings and pies and peaches and cream. He began to eat.

"Is it to your liking?" asked the captain.

"Well enough," said Matilda's uncle, one arm still cradling the churn.

"But I wish there was a little more salt."

Chinkelly chunk . . . chunk . . .

The churn's handle began to turn, slowly at first.

"STOP!" shrieked the uncle, clinging to the handle. "STOP!"

Chunkelly chink . . . chinkelly chunk . . .

The handle went faster.

The uncle was very pale. Nothing he did, nothing he said made the handle stop turning. Salt spilled out, more and more and more.

The ship's cabin filled with salt. All the crew swept and tossed the salt overboard as the deck was heaped with salt, but it was no use. The deck was piled high. The 't reached the lowest sails, then the highest—and higher. The ship reeled and heeled, and the ship's crew leaped into a little boat and rowed furiously away across the sea.

The ship he sighed and sank, down to sands at the

very bottom of the ocean. No one
ever saw the uncle again, but
down in the dark depths of the
wide and rolling sea, as
blue and as green as a
kingfisher's wing, the
churn went on turning.
*Chinkelly chunk,
chunkelly chink . . .*

A few days later, Matilda was sitting at the edge of the sea, dabbling her hand in the water. "That's odd," said Matilda, as she licked her fingers. "I do believe the sea tastes different."

"What does it taste of?" asked her littlest sister.

"Well," Matilda said, "it tastes of salt."

And so it did . . .

and so it does . . .

and so it always will.